LIFE CYCLE OF A...

Silkworm

Revised and Updated

Ron Fridell
and
Patricia Walsh

Heinemann Library
Chicago, Illinois

www.heinemannraintree.com

Visit our website to find out
more information about
Heinemann-Raintree books.

To order:

 Phone 888-454-2279

Visit www.heinemannraintree.com
to browse our catalog and order online.

Edited by Adrian Vigliano, Harriet Milles, and Diyan Leake
Designed by Kimberly R. Miracle and Tony Miracle
Original illustrations ©Capstone Global Library Limited
 2001, 2009
Illustrated by Alan Fraser
Picture research by Tracy Cummins and Heather Mauldin
Originated by Chroma Graphics (Overseas) Pte. Ltd.
Printed in China by South China Printing Company Ltd.

13 12 11 10 09
10 9 8 7 6 5 4 3 2 1

New edition ISBNs: 978 1 4329 2528 4 (hardcover)
                    978 1 4329 2545 1 (paperback)

**The Library of Congress has cataloged the first edition
as follows:**
Fridell, Ron.
 Life cycle of a silkworm / by Ron Fridell, Patricia Walsh.
  p. cm.
 Includes bibliographical references and index.
  ISBN 1-58810-094-4
  1. Silkworm—Life cycles—Juvenile literature. [1.
Silkworms.]
  I. Title: Silkworm. II. Walsh, Patricia, 1951- III. Title.
 SF542.5 .F75 2001
 638.2—dc21
            00-011235

Acknowledgments
The author and publishers are grateful to the following for
permission to reproduce copyright material: ©Em Ahart pp.
12, **21**; Corbis pp. **14**, **15**, **28 bottom** (©Gallo Images/Anthony
Bannister), **26** (©Wolfgang Kaehler); Getty Images pp. **10**, **28
top right** (©Keren Su), **24** (©Dennis Johnson); ©James Kalisch
p. **29 top right**; ©Dwight Kuhn pp. **6**, **8**, **16**, **19**, **28 top left**, **29
top left**; Photolibrary pp. **20**, **29 bottom** (©Paul Beard)Photo
Researchers Inc. p. **23** (©S. Nagendra); Photoshot pp. **7**, **13**, **22**,
(©Bruce Coleman/E.R. Degginger); Shutterstock pp. **5** (©July
Flower), **11** (©sf2301420max), **25** (©Joris Van Den Heuvel) **27**
(©Naomi Hasegawa); University of Nebraska pp. **4**, **9**, **17**, **18**
(©James Kalisch).

Cover photograph of a silkworm reproduced with permission
of age fotostock (©San Rostro).

Every effort has been made to contact copyright holders of
any material reproduced in this book. Any omissions will
be rectified in subsequent printings if notice is given to the
publisher.

We would like to thank Michael Bright for his invaluable help
in the preparation of this book.

Contents

Some words are shown in bold, **like this**. You can find out what they mean by looking in the glossary.

Meet the Silkworms

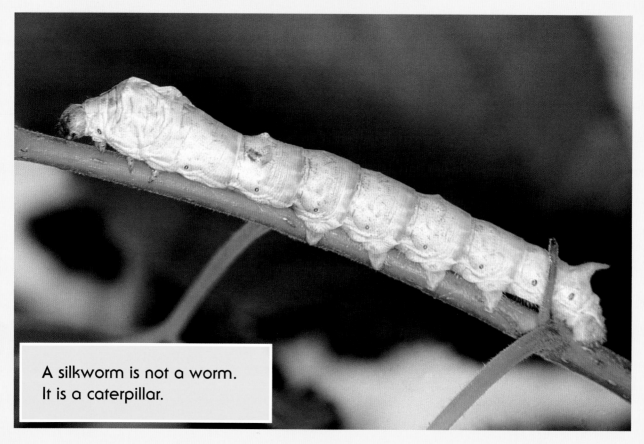

A silkworm is not a worm.
It is a caterpillar.

A silkworm is an **insect**. It looks like
it has many legs, but only six are true
legs. It uses the other ten legs to cling
to plants.

1 day

3 weeks

5-7 weeks

Many years ago, silkworms lived in the wild. Today, most silkworms are **domesticated**. They live only on silk farms.

Silk farmers **breed** silkworms to get the silk thread they make.

Egg

The female silk moth lays hundreds of eggs.

The silkworm begins life in a tiny egg. The egg is one of about 300 sticky, yellow eggs laid by the female silk **moth**.

1 day

3 weeks

5-7 weeks

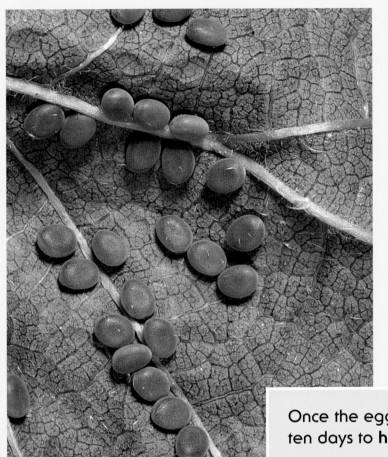

The egg needs to stay cold for a few weeks. Then the egg is warmed up and its center turns black.

Once the egg is warm, it takes about ten days to **hatch**.

Hatching

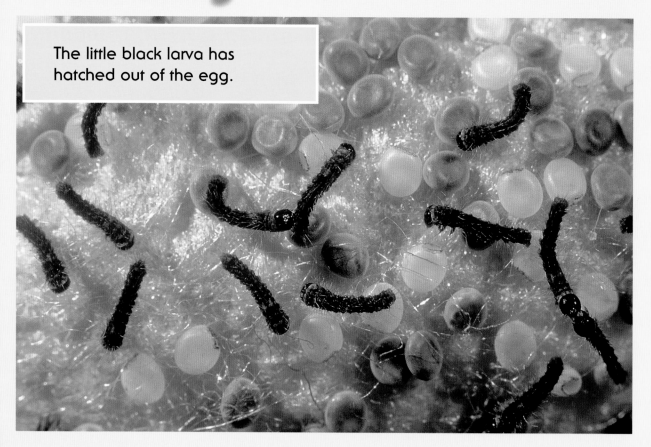

The little black larva has hatched out of the egg.

When the tiny silkworm **larva** is ready to **hatch**, it bites a hole in the egg. Then it wriggles out.

1 day

3 weeks

5-7 weeks

The new larva quickly starts to eat.

The newly hatched silkworm larva looks like a tiny black string. At first it is too weak to crawl very far, but it is ready to eat.

8 weeks

10 weeks

11 weeks

Larva

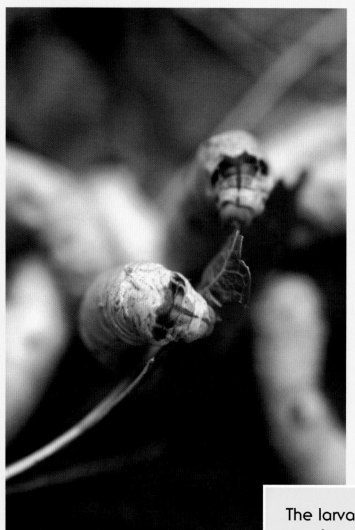

The new **larva** needs to have its food close by. In a few days, the larva will be stronger. It will crawl from leaf to leaf.

The larva eats only mulberry tree leaves.

1 day

3 weeks

5-7 weeks

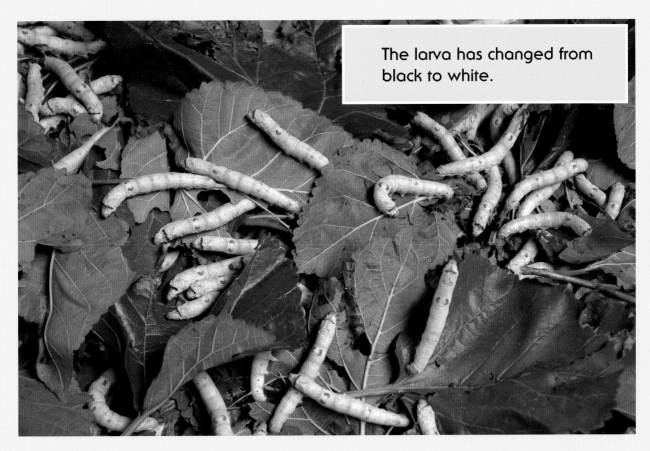

The larva has changed from black to white.

The larva eats a lot of mulberry leaves. It does not drink water. It gets enough **moisture** from the leaves.

8 weeks

10 weeks

11 weeks

Molting

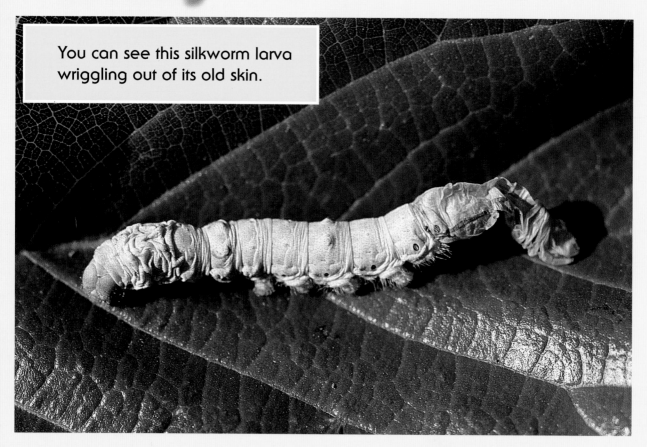

You can see this silkworm larva wriggling out of its old skin.

The **larva's** skin does not stretch as it grows. To get bigger, a silkworm must **molt**. The old skin splits. The silkworm wriggles out wearing its new skin.

1 day

3 weeks

5-7 weeks

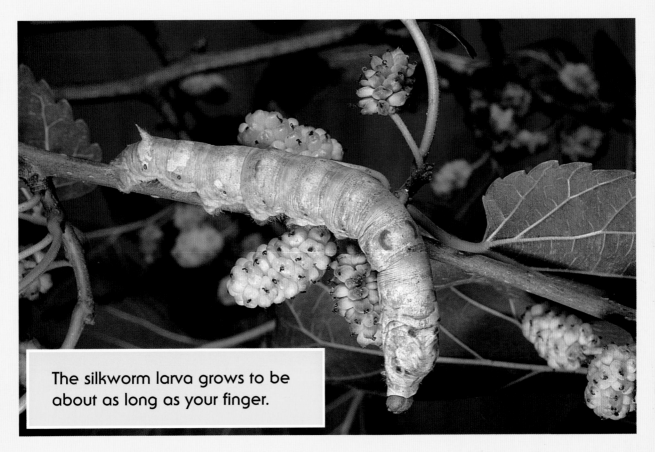

The silkworm larva grows to be about as long as your finger.

The larva molts four times. After the fourth molt, the larva eats even more mulberry leaves than it did before.

8 weeks

10 weeks

11 weeks

Spinning the Cocoon

The silkworm starts to spin a silk thread.

The **larva** is ready to spin a **cocoon**. It makes its cocoon from one long, sticky silk thread that comes from its mouth.

1 day

3 weeks

5-7 weeks

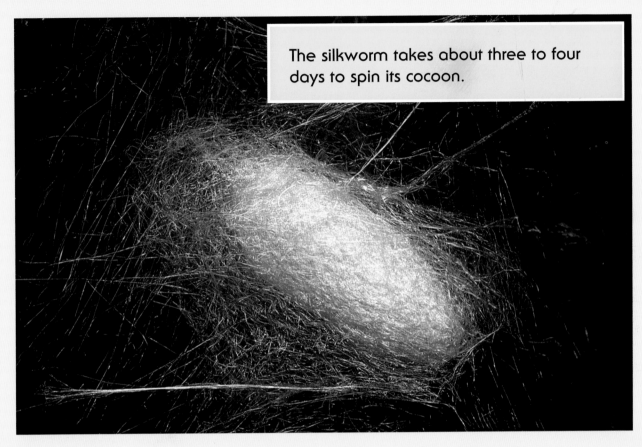

The silkworm takes about three to four days to spin its cocoon.

First the larva spins a silk web. Then it spins and spins for three days. It spins a silk cocoon around itself.

8 weeks

10 weeks

11 weeks

Pupa

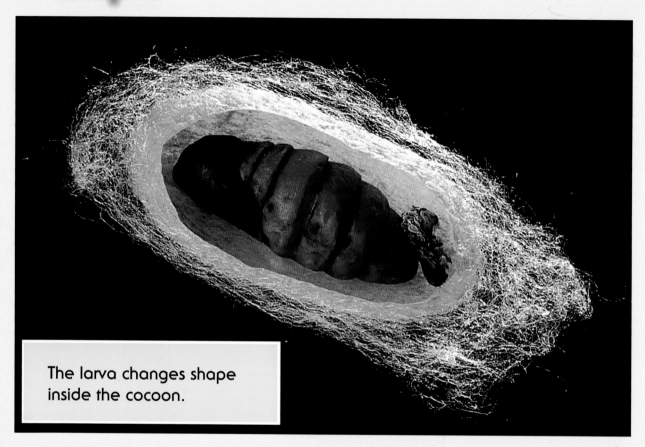

The larva changes shape inside the cocoon.

Inside the **cocoon**, the **larva molts** one last time. This time it changes to a brown **pupa** with a hard shell.

1 day

3 weeks

5-7 weeks

It is time for the moth to leave the cocoon.

After two weeks the shell splits. The pupa has turned into a silk **moth**. The moth spits a special liquid. The liquid wets the inside of the cocoon, and makes a hole.

8 weeks

10 weeks

11 weeks

Leaving the Cocoon

The moth looks very different from the silkworm it used to be.

The **pupa** has changed into a white adult silk **moth**. The moth has wings and large eyes. On its head there are two **antennae** that look like feathers.

1 day

3 weeks

5-7 weeks

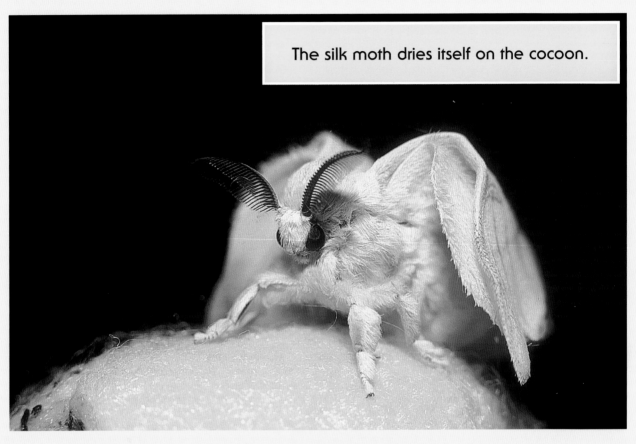

The silk moth dries itself on the cocoon.

The silk moth pulls itself through the hole in the **cocoon**. In about an hour, its damp wings unfold and dry.

8 weeks

10 weeks

11 weeks

Silk Moth

The silk **moth** has six legs and two **antennae**. It also has four wings. But a **domesticated** moth cannot fly.

The silk moth is about 2 inches (3–5 centimeters) wide.

1 day

3 weeks

5-7 weeks

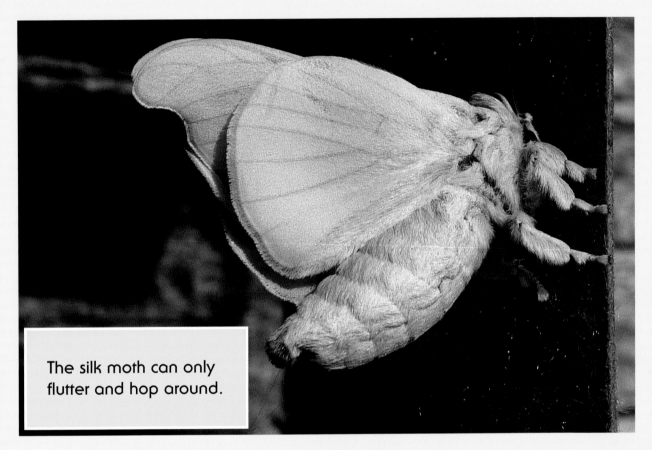

The silk moth can only flutter and hop around.

For the next few days, the silk moth does not eat or drink anything.

Mating

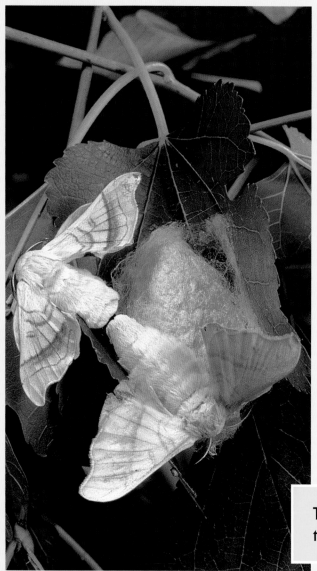

Soon after coming out of the **cocoon**, the female **moth** gives off a **scent**. This helps a male moth to find her. Then they **mate**.

The female silk moth is bigger than the male.

1 day

3 weeks

5-7 weeks

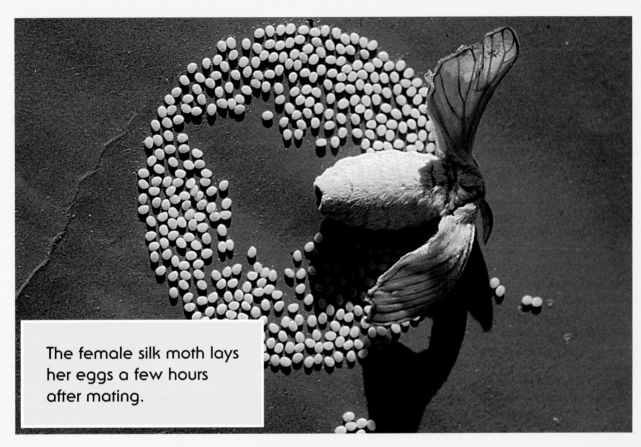

The female silk moth lays her eggs a few hours after mating.

After mating, the male moth dies. When the female moth has laid her eggs, she will die, too.

8 weeks

10 weeks

11 weeks

Silk from Silkworms

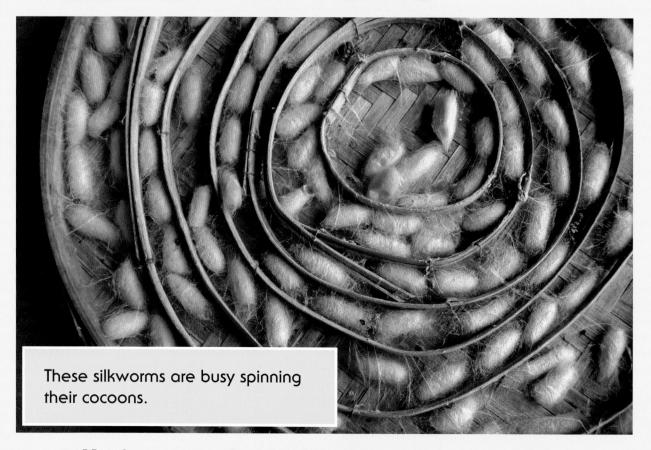

These silkworms are busy spinning their cocoons.

Silk farmers **breed** silkworms for their **cocoons**. The silk thread of the cocoons is woven into silk cloth.

1 day

3 weeks

5-7 weeks

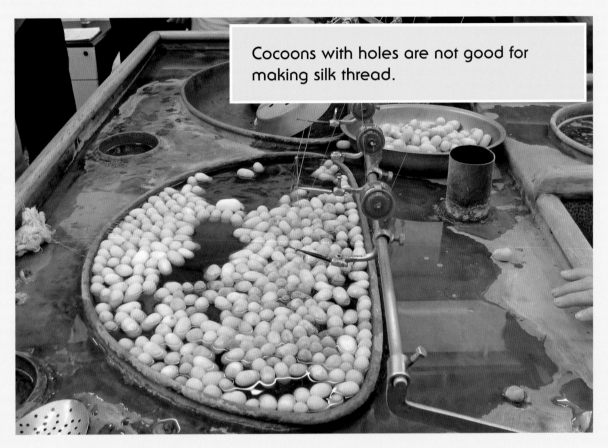

Cocoons with holes are not good for making silk thread.

On silk farms, most **pupas** never change into **moths**. If moths were allowed to come out of the cocoons, there would be holes in the cocoons.

8 weeks

10 weeks

11 weeks

Making Silk Cloth

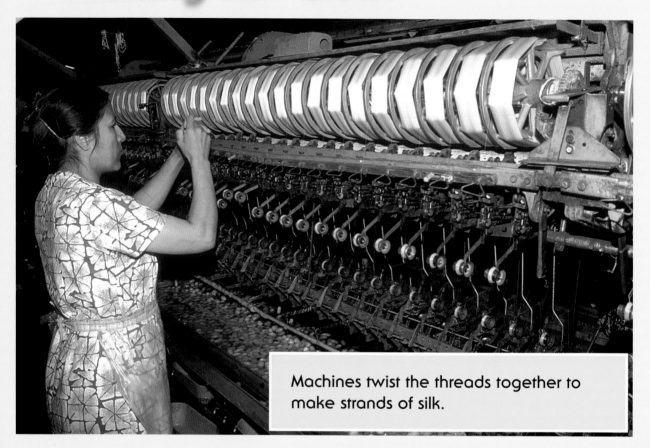

Machines twist the threads together to make strands of silk.

The long, white, silk thread from the **cocoon** is as thin as a spiderweb. It is unwound from the cocoon.

1 day

3 weeks

5-7 weeks

The **strands** of silk are woven into silk cloth. The cloth can be **dyed** any color to make beautiful clothes.

These Japanese girls are wearing dresses made of silk cloth.

8 weeks

10 weeks

11 weeks

Life Cycle

Egg

Larva

Cocoon

Pupa

Leaving the cocoon

Silk moth

Fact File

- The silkworm **larva** moves its head backwards and forwards in a figure-of-eight pattern as it spins its **cocoon**.

- It takes 110 cocoons to make a silk tie. It takes 630 cocoons to make a silk shirt.

- Other kinds of **moths** can fly to escape **predators**. A **domesticated** silk moth has no predators, so it does not fly.

- A single thread of silk from a silkworm's cocoon can be one mile long. That is about as long as 17 football fields laid end to end.

- A single thread of silk is stronger than the same size thread of some types of steel.

Glossary

antenna   long, thin feeler on an insect's head. (More than one are called antennae.)

cocoon   silken case that protects the pupa inside it

breed   to care for an animal or plant until it is fully grown

domesticated   cared for by humans

dye   change the color of fabric

hatch   come out of an egg

insect   small animal that has six legs, a body with three parts, and wings

larva   caterpillar-like stage of an insect's life when it eats and grows

mate   when a male and female come together to make babies

moisture   water, wetness

moth   insect with a thick body and four wide wings. A moth is similar to a butterfly.

molt   shed the outer skin

predator   animal that eats other animals

pupa   resting stage in an insect's life, between larva and adult

scent   odor or smell

strand   thread or string

More Books to Read

Guillain, Charlotte and Sue Barraclough. *Investigate: Life Cycles.* Chicago: Heinemann Library, 2008.

Oxlade, Chris. *How We Use: Silk.* Chicago: Raintree, 2005.

Index